AMOS

THE STORY OF
AN OLD DOG
AND HIS COUCH

by SUSAN SELIGSON
and HOWIE SCHNEIDER

Joy Street Books
Little, Brown and Company
Boston   Toronto

Dedicated to old dogs everywhere

A Floyd Yearout Book

316 Wellesley Street, Weston, Massachusetts 02193

First Edition

Library of Congress Cataloging-in-Publication Data
Schneider, Howie, 1930-
  Amos: The story of an old dog and his couch.
  Summary: An old dog finds adventure when he discovers that his favorite
couch has a motor and can be driven.
  [1. Dogs — Fiction. 2. Humorous stories] I. Seligson, Susan. II. Title.
PZ7.S3635Am 1987   [E]   87-2813
ISBN 0-316-77404-9

Published simultaneously in Canada
by Little, Brown & Company (Canada) Limited

Printed in Italy

Amos is an old dog

who lives on an old couch

in an old house

that used to be
filled with activity.

Once the kids were all grown up and had moved away,
things were kind of quiet.

Mr. and Mrs. Bobson went out a lot . . .

but they never
took Amos with them
anymore.

"Where do they go?" Amos wondered.
"If only I could go along," he thought.

One day after the Bobsons had gone out,
Amos was awakened by a loud,
          persistent BUZZZZZZZ.

He hadn't caught a fly in years,
but he decided to give it a try.

He tried and he tried.
Finally, he went after it with his paw.

He missed the fly but had hit something else,

for suddenly . . .

. . . the couch MOVED!
Amos hit the cushion again.
The couch seemed to come alive.

He tried it again   and again.

Finally, he backed the couch up

. . . very slowly . . . and guided it into place.

Amos could not remember when he had been so tired . . .
or so happy.

The next morning
Amos could hardly wait for the
Bobsons to leave.

As soon as they were gone,
he started up his couch and
threw it into gear.

He shot out the door just in time to spot the Bobsons
pulling out of the driveway.

So he
followed them . . .

right out
into traffic.

He managed to stay with them all the way
to the supermarket.
"Probably gonna buy me some chicken," he thought,
and waited patiently for their return.

He didn't mind waiting.
He had plenty of company.

Pretty soon
the Bobsons
were back.

Amos started up his couch and
followed the Bobsons out of the parking lot.

Next they stopped at a yard sale.

Amos
had to think
fast.

"Say, that looks just like our couch," said
Mr. Bobson. "Oh, it couldn't be," said Mrs. Bobson.
"Our couch is home with Amos on it."

Amos decided he had taken enough chances
for one day. When the Bobsons drove off on their
next errand, he headed straight for home.

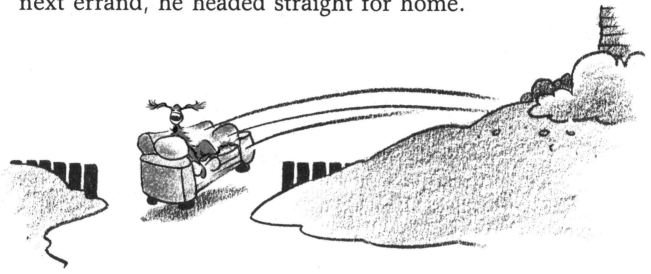

When the Bobsons got back, they found Amos
stretched out on his couch as usual . . .

looking a bit
more tired than
usual.

That night they all had chicken,
just as Amos knew they would.

The next morning Amos wasted no time.
As soon as he heard the Bobsons start their motor,
he started his . . .

and was on his way.

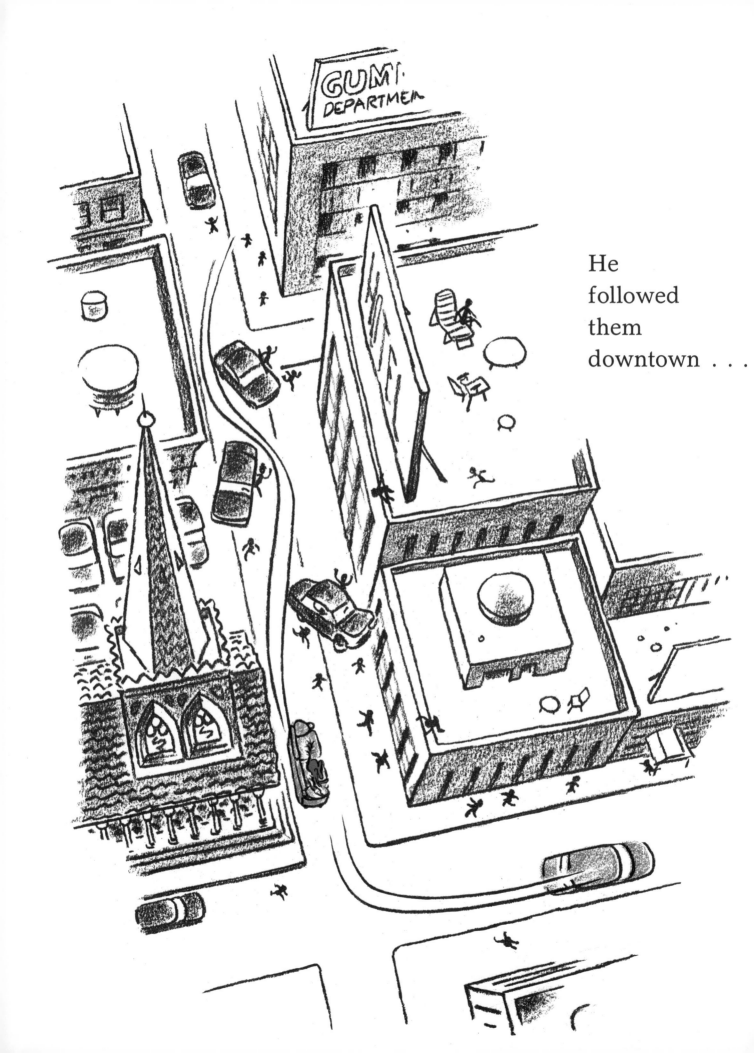

He
followed
them
downtown . . .

over
the
bridge

through
the zoo . . .

past the playground.

Amos began to grow
tired and hungry . . . so
he headed for home.

On the way he stopped
to make a few friends.

He
stopped
again

to make a few more friends . . .

and a few more.

Suddenly Amos realized it was getting late.
"I'd better hurry," he thought.

But what Amos hadn't thought about
(and what dog **does** think about such things ?)
was rush hour traffic . . .

that was bumper to bumper to couch to bumper.

He would never get home
before the Bobsons
unless they were stuck
in traffic, too.

But they weren't.

"Where on earth could he be?"

He
hadn't
touched
his
food.

His toys were
where they had
always been . . .
under his couch.

But where **was** the couch?

The Bobsons began to fear they might never see Amos again.

But rush hour doesn't last forever.

AMOS

Amos needn't have worried.
The Bobsons were just happy to see him.
"So that's your secret," they said.

From then on Amos was the happiest dog in the world because

the Bobsons took him everywhere they went.

And every once in a while . . .

Amos took them someplace, too!